Magic
Ballerin
The Magic *

Welcome to the world of Enchantia!

I have always loved to dance. The captivating
music and wonderful stories of ballet are so
inspiring. So come with me and let's follow
Delphie on her magical adventures in
Enchantia, where the stories of dance will
take you on a very special journey.

P.S. Turn to the back to learn a special
dance step from me. . . .

Special thanks to
Linda Chapman and
Katie May

Harper Trophy® is a registered trademark of HarperCollins
Publishers.

Magic Ballerina: The Magic Ballet Shoes
Text copyright © 2009 by Darcey Bussell
Illustrations copyright © 2009 by Katie May
All rights reserved. Printed in the United States of America.
No part of this book may be used or reproduced in any manner
whatsoever without written permission except in the case of brief
quotations embodied in critical articles and reviews. For information
address HarperCollins Children's Books, a division of HarperCollins
Publishers, 1350 Avenue of the Americas, New York, NY 10019.
www.harpercollinschildrens.com

Library of Congress catalog card number: 2008939058
ISBN 978-0-06-173335-2

09 10 11 12 13 CG/CW 10 9 8 7 6 5 4 3 2 1
❖
First published in Great Britain by HarperCollins Children's
Books, 2008
First U.S. edition, 2009

Magic Ballerina

The Magic Ballet Shoes

Darcey Bussell

HarperTrophy®
An Imprint of HarperCollinsPublishers

ENCH

Royal Palace

Sugar Plum Fairy's Cottage

The Village

The Land of SWEETS

THEATER

Theater

To Phoebe and Zoe, as they are the inspiration behind Magic Ballerina.

Contents

Prologue

In the soft, pale light, the girl stood
with her head bent and her hands
held lightly in front of her.
There was a moment's silence, and then
the first notes of the music began.
For as long as the girl could remember,
music had seemed to tell her of
another world—a magical, exciting
world—that lay far, far away.
She always felt if she could just
close her eyes and lose herself,
then she would get there.
Maybe this time. As the music
swirled inside her, she swept
her arms above her head, rose on to
her toes, and began to dance. . . .

Madame Zarakova's School of Ballet

Delphie hurried home, her breath freezing in the snowy night air. The houses on either side of the road had their curtains drawn—except for one: a big double-fronted house with iron railings and a gate. Two stone steps led up to the door, and light streamed out of the windows. As the snowflakes landed softly on Delphie's shoulders, she looked longingly at the brass plate, just as she had for the last four weeks since it had been open: *Madame Zarakova's School of Ballet.*

A car drew up outside and two girls jumped out. They were about nine—the same age as Delphie—and had their hair tied back in neat buns.

"Come on, we're going to be late!" one of

them called as they ran through the gate and opened the front door. "Madame Za-Za will be upset!"

For a moment, Delphie caught sight of a long wide hallway with white walls and wooden floors before the heavy door banged shut behind them.

Delphie felt a wave of longing so strong it hurt. She wanted to be inside the ballet school about to have a dance lesson. She was ballet-crazy, but her parents had always put off Delphie having lessons.

"Maybe when you're a bit older," her mom had said, kissing Delphie's long dark hair. "The nearest dance school is on the other side of town. It's too far to take you every week."

But Delphie hadn't been put off. She had

borrowed books from the library and
practiced ballet exercises almost every day.
And she danced all the time—in the house,
in the garden—
she wasn't even
embarrassed to
dance on the
street! She loved
the feeling of
spinning,
moving,
jumping.
It was hard to
explain but,
although she
had never had
any lessons,

inside she just felt that she knew what it was like to be a real ballerina.

And now Madame Zarakova's ballet school had opened on the very street she lived. But even that hadn't helped her. Delphie did understand. After all, money was tight in their house.

"I'm sorry, sweetheart," Mrs. Durand, Delphie's mother, had sighed. "We just can't afford to send you there."

Standing by the railings now, Delphie could hear the faint sounds of a piano tinkling and, through the branches, she could see light from the big windows falling

into the front garden. Shivering, she pulled
her coat closer around her as she looked
over the railings.

The music and lights seemed to be calling
her nearer. Slipping through the gate, she
crept over to the house, peering in through
the window. The room inside was large,
with mirrors on each of the four walls. Eight
girls, all about the same age, were holding
lightly to the *barre*, a wooden pole that was
fixed around the wall of the room. They
were all dressed in pink leotards with a
ribbon around their waists, pale socks, and
satin ballet shoes with ribbons crossed
neatly around their ankles.

They were gracefully bending and
straightening their knees out over their toes.

"*Pliés,*" Delphie sighed longingly,
recognizing them from one of her books.
Oh, if only she could be in there with them.

Madame Za-Za was walking around the room, talking to the girls and correcting a leg position here, an arm position there. She held her own body erect, and her gray-streaked brown hair was pulled back in a bun. As Delphie watched, the girls began a different exercise, pointing their toes and sliding their legs to the back, front, and side. *Battements tendu*, thought Delphie. All the girls looked good, but there was one dark-haired girl who looked very graceful and seemed to find everything easy.

Next the girls began sliding the foot that was farthest from the *barre* and lifting it off the floor, stretching out as far as they could and holding their free arm out to the side.

Delphie couldn't resist. She began to join in.

Holding on to the windowsill,
she performed the
movement in time with
the girls inside.

Sweeping her arm
and leg to the side, she
held them in perfect
position, her toe pointed
and heel raised from the
ground. They moved
into practicing quick,
light movements.

Madame Za-Za said something to the girls
and left the room. The class kept working.
Feeling very happy, Delphie continued to
copy them. It was almost like being in there.

Then, suddenly, the front door swung

open and a voice called out.
"You, girl! What are you
doing?"

Delphie jumped in shock
and swung around. She
had been concentrating so
hard on the dancing that
she hadn't heard the door
opening. It was Madame
Za-Za standing on the
top step, staring at her!

Delphie froze to the
spot. "I . . . I'm really sorry! I just wanted to
have a look."

"Come here, child!" Madame Za-Za called.

And with just a moment's hesitation,
Delphie hurried up the steps.

The Red Ballet Shoes

"Come inside, child," Madame Za-Za said. "What is your name?"

"Delphie Durand." Delphie felt tears prickling her eyes. She was sure she was about to be lectured. She blinked quickly; she hated crying in front of people.

"I saw you through the window,"

Madame Za-Za said to her. "Where do you learn ballet?"

Delphie was very surprised by the question. "I . . . I don't go to classes," she answered. "I just read about it in books and practice at home."

"I see." Madame Za-Za looked at her for a moment. "Well, why don't you come in?"

"Come in?" Delphie echoed.

Madame Za-Za nodded. "It's cold out here and I think you would like to have a look around. Am I right?"

"Yes!" Delphie gasped. "I'd love to see inside."

"Come, then."

Walking in a daze, Delphie followed Madame Za-Za inside the school. They went down the warm, brightly lit corridor. "Here we have the dance studios," Madame Za-Za explained, pointing to two rooms, one on either side.

"Wow!" Delphie breathed.

Madame Za-Za looked thoughtfully at her. "Do you have any ballet shoes, child?"

"No," Delphie replied. She always just danced in bare feet.

Madame Za-Za gave a small nod and then

set off down a dark corridor, opening a door
at the end that led into a small storeroom.
The walls were covered with shelves piled
high with boxes, dusty books, ballet
costumes, and what looked like a chest full
of new ballet leotards and socks.

Madame Za-Za went into the room and
took an old, battered box down from a high
shelf.

As Delphie watched, Madame Za-Za
opened the lid to reveal a pair of old red
leather ballet shoes with red ribbons, nestling
among yellowing tissue paper. The leather
was slightly crinkly, the insides of the shoes a
deep cream. They were worn and slightly
shabby but as Delphie looked at them, she
felt a sudden urge to reach into the box.

Her feet tingled as if they wanted to try the shoes on.

Unable to stop herself, she touched the soft red leather. Then, realizing what she was doing, she pulled her hand back.

She looked up to see Madame Za-Za studying her face, her expression unreadable.

"Do you like them?" Madame Za-Za asked.
"Oh, yes," Delphie breathed. The ballet
shoes might be old but
they were beautiful.
"Would you like
to borrow them,
child?" Madame
Za-Za asked gently.

"Borrow them!" Delphie stared in
surprise. "But why would you lend them to
me? I don't even come here to classes."

"If you like, you can come back tomorrow
and join in with the class you were watching,"
Madame Za-Za said.

Delphie could hardly believe her ears.
"But . . . but . . . well, I'd love to, but Mom
and Dad can't afford for me to have lessons."

She blushed as she admitted the truth.

Madame Za-Za waved her hand
dismissively. "Money does not matter.
Just come tomorrow as I ask." Her eyes
met Delphie's. "I will teach you for free."

Delphie's mind spun.

"Go home now and tell your parents
what I have said. They may call me if
they have any questions." Madame Za-Za
gave her the box with the ballet shoes
and then turned and took a brand-new
pink leotard and socks out of the chest near
the door. "Bring these clothes and the shoes
to wear tomorrow."

Delphie looked down at the box in
her arms. "What if the shoes don't
fit me?"

Madame Za-Za gave a mysterious smile.
"Oh, I don't think there will be a problem
with that. I think you will find them the
perfect size. They have been waiting for the
right person to come along, and something
tells me you might be that person."

Her eyes stared deep into Delphie's.
"They are very special shoes, Delphie. I

hope one day you find out just how special they are." Suddenly her tone became brisker. "Now, I must return to class. I will see you tomorrow, ready and changed for half past four sharp."

"Thank you!" Delphie gasped.

Almost before she knew it, she was following Madame Za-Za back down the corridor and then she was back outside in the snow again. But Delphie didn't feel cold. Excitement raced through her as she hugged the shoes to her chest. She rushed home to tell her mom. She was going to start ballet classes tomorrow. She couldn't wait!

The Ballet Class

Delphie could hardly concentrate in school at all the next day. All she could think about was her first ballet lesson. She was at Madame Za-Za's school by four o'clock and had changed twenty minutes before the class was due to start.

As Delphie tied her long hair back into a bun, she looked at herself in the mirror and

couldn't stop grinning. She
looked just like the girls
she had been watching the
day before. Well, apart
from the fact that her shoes
were red instead of pale pink, but
Delphie didn't care about that. They were
beautifully soft and they fit her perfectly,
just as Madame Za-Za had said they would.

Other girls started to arrive. The two who
Delphie had seen running into the ballet
school the day before were the first to get
there. "Who are you?" one of them asked
curiously.

"I'm Delphie," she replied.

"Are you just starting lessons here?" the
other girl asked.

Delphie nodded.

"Well, I'm Poppy," the first girl said. "And this is Lola."

"Hi-ya, Delphie." Lola said with a smile.

Other girls started to pile in who were just as friendly. At half past four they all went into the dance studio, where Madame Za-Za was waiting for them.

They began with *pliés* at the *barre*. Delphie concentrated hard, trying to remember everything she had read in her books.

As she followed Madame Za-Za's instructions, she felt herself relax, and soon it was just as if she was practicing in her bedroom at home—but a hundred times better because she was in a real ballet class.

Madame Za-Za kept telling them to keep their heads up and to smile, but Delphie didn't find that difficult at all.

The girls moved from the *barre* to working

in the center of the room. They went through the same exercises again and then practiced arm movements, different poses, and turns called pirouettes.

As they neared the end of the class, Madame Za-Za explained to Delphie that the class had been learning a dance from a ballet called *The Nutcracker*.

Delphie had read about *The Nutcracker*— a girl called Clara was given a nutcracker who looked like a soldier as a Christmas present by her uncle. Clara loved her new toy so much that she crept downstairs when everyone was in bed and danced with him before falling asleep.

"I think you had better just watch this part of the class, Delphie," Madame Za-Za said to her. "The others have been learning the dance for a while now."

Delphie sat, feeling nervous, as the other eight girls took turns to hold a wooden doll that looked like a toy soldier and dance Clara's dance. The dark-haired girl, who Delphie had found out was called

Sukie, was the last to go. She moved very gracefully and didn't wobble on any of the positions she held. Her turns were easy and smooth,

35

and her arms and head always seemed to be held perfectly in position. But even so, there was something that wasn't quite right. *What is it?* Delphie wondered.

Madame Za-Za was watching from near the piano. As Sukie finished and smiled, Madame Za-Za walked forward, shaking her head. "No, Sukie, your hands, your arms, your placing were all good, but you are supposed to love the doll you are holding. I did not believe that when I watched you."

Delphie realized she knew exactly what Madame Za-Za meant. Although Sukie's dancing had looked wonderful, she hadn't made Delphie feel like she was really watching Clara.

Madame Za-Za turned to all the girls. "Ballet is about much more than just dancing—the real magic comes from telling a story and making the audience believe in that story." Her eyes looked straight into Delphie's. "Never forget that—always believe in it."

Delphie felt a longing to do the dance herself. She wanted to be up there, wanted Madame Za-Za to be watching her, but it was too late—it was the end of the class.

As soon as she had changed, Delphie ran all the way home. She couldn't wait to tell her parents about the class. This had been the best day of her life!

That night, when Delphie went to bed, she relived every moment of the class. *I'll have to learn the dance the others were doing*, she thought, picking up a book that was lying on her bedside table that told all the stories from the ballet.

Delphie turned to the chapter on *The Nutcracker*. She wanted to know what happened after Clara's dance. She read how, in the story, Clara dreams that the Nutcracker has come to life. Then the evil King Rat, with his army of mice, tries to fight the Nutcracker. Clara helps to defeat King Rat by throwing her slipper at his head, which knocks him out. Then the

Nutcracker changes into a handsome prince and takes Clara on a magical journey to the Land of Snow and the Land of Sweets. She meets the Sugar Plum Fairy and lots of other amazing characters, like the snowflakes and Jack Frost, the Rose Fairy and the Arabian dancers.

Delphie sighed happily as she read the end of the story. Turning off the light, she snuggled down in bed, imagining herself dancing Clara's dance. Suddenly she heard a faint tinkling sound and some faraway music. What was that?

She listened hard. There it was again. She sat up in bed.

The red ballet shoes were glittering and sparkling in the dark!

A Magical Land

Delphie stared at the twinkling shoes and then leaped out of bed. She was about to run out of the room to get her mother when Madame Za-Za's voice came back to her: *They are very special shoes, Delphie. I hope one day you find out just how special they are.*

Something seemed to be telling Delphie to stay—not to go. She reached out and touched the shoes. Her fingers seemed to spark with a tiny electric shock, and suddenly she felt as if she just had to put them on.

She picked up the left shoe. As she slipped it on, her foot felt light and sparkly. She put the other shoe on and, as she tied the ribbons, the tingling spread through her whole body. Delphie stood up and then gasped as suddenly the shoes began to make her pirouette around and around. . . .

Delphie whirled, her bedroom blurring into a sparkling haze of colors. She cried out. *What was happening?*

Then the colors faded and she found herself on a seat. She looked around in astonishment. She was in a large, empty theater. In front of her there was an enormous stage with red curtains, shut tight. The lights began to go down and, before Delphie's eyes, the curtains rose.

A scene of a village street appeared with a large mountain behind it. On the slope of the mountain, a dark castle was painted. Feeling sure that she must be dreaming, Delphie looked at the stage. A fairy in a pale-lilac tutu was sitting on a tree stump, her hands covering her face.

Behind her there were dancers dressed as multicolored flowers, two people in Russian costumes, a girl in a long red Spanish dress, and a clown. Delphie wondered if this was the beginning of some sort of show, but as she looked more closely, she realized that the fairy was crying.

Delphie got to her feet and went down the aisle that led up to the stage. "Hello!" she called. Her voice sounded loud in the silence of the theater.

The fairy jumped in surprise. "Who are you?"

"My name's Delphie," Delphie replied. "Who are you?"

"I'm the Sugar Plum Fairy," she said.

"You mean you're dancing the part of the Sugar Plum Fairy in *The Nutcracker*," Delphie said, feeling confused.

"No, I really am the Sugar Plum Fairy." The ballerina stood up, her sparkling tutu catching the lights on the stage. "People call me Sugar for short. This is the entrance to the Land of Enchantia—the land where the characters from all the different ballets live." She looked curiously at Delphie. "Where have you come from?"

"From . . . from my bedroom," Delphie stammered. "My ballet shoes started to sparkle, so I put them on and I ended up here."

"You've got the magic ballet shoes!" Sugar breathed. "I've heard about those. Every so often they are given to someone who really loves ballet and they bring that person to Enchantia. It happens whenever there's a problem here."

Delphie stared at her. "Madame Za-Za—the person who gave them to me—said they were special. She must have meant they were magic." Delphie's eyes widened and she looked around wonderingly. "So this is all real. It's not a dream." She remembered something the Sugar Plum Fairy had just said. "You said the shoes work when there's a problem."

Sugar nodded. "Yes, and we have a very big problem right now. The people in Enchantia usually live happily together and

dance all day. But not anymore." Her blue
eyes welled up with tears. "Evil King Rat
has stopped everyone from dancing."

"King Rat?" Delphie echoed, thinking
back to the villain of the ballet she'd been
reading about before she
went to bed.

Sugar nodded sadly.
"He hates dancing. He's
captured the Nutcracker
and turned him into a
wooden toy. Without the

magic of the Nutcracker, no one in
Enchantia can dance—all the toys have
become lifeless. The sweets have become
just sweets again, and the snowflakes have
frozen. I can't dance either. Look at this!"

She stood up and, with a
graceful lift of her arms,
rose onto her pointes.
She only managed to
dance three steps
forward before she
wobbled over. "The
magic of the dance has
gone. The only way to
stop King Rat is to free
the Nutcracker and bring
him back to life again. But King Rat is
keeping him prisoner in his castle, and
everyone's too scared to go there."

Delphie thought how awful it would be
not to be able to dance. "I'll help you," she
said eagerly.

"It could be very dangerous," Sugar warned. "The castle is guarded by King Rat's army of mice. They're big and carry swords and are very fierce."

"I don't care," said Delphie bravely. "I want to help you free the Nutcracker!"

"Oh, thank you!" Sugar grabbed Delphie's hands. "Thank you so much!"

"So, how do we get to the castle?" Delphie asked.

Sugar smiled. "By magic, of course!"

Off to the Castle!

Sugar pulled a silver wand out of a pocket of her tutu and waved it in the air. Purple sparks flew out and swirled around them in a haze. Delphie felt herself pirouetting around three times in the air before she landed on her feet as the sparkles cleared.

Delphie gasped. They were no longer on the stage but standing in the woods with fallen branches and leaves beneath their feet. The air smelled horrible—of rotten fruit and old food.

"That's King Rat's castle," whispered Sugar, pointing through the trees. Delphie could see a dark shape looming ahead of them, its stone turrets silhouetted against the sky.

Two mice, a bit taller than Delphie, were guarding the big wooden door that led into the castle. They were standing on their back legs and wore swords slung through leather belts. Their eyes were beady and their snouts were long.

"What's that awful smell?" Delphie whispered back.

"King Rat gets his mice to bring great piles of garbage here so he can rummage around in them and eat to his heart's content. He loves it."

Sugar waved her wand. There was a tinkle of music, and two sugarcoated plums appeared in her hand. "These should help take the smell away. Put one in your pocket." She handed one to Delphie.

Delphie breathed in a
wave of sweetness—
icing, sugar, cotton
candy, fresh plums, and
peaches. "That's much

better!" She slipped the sugarplum into
her pocket and looked around. "How are
we going to get into the castle to rescue
the Nutcracker?"

"I don't know," said Sugar. "I can use
my magic to travel around Enchantia,
but I can't use it to get inside King Rat's
castle. His powers are much stronger
than mine."

Delphie crept forward to the edge of the
trees. How were they going to get in?

Suddenly both mice sniffed the air.

"Sugarplums!" said the mouse on the left. He was tall and thin with very pointed teeth. "I smell sugarplums!"

"Me too," said the other mouse, who was smaller and fatter with tiny eyes.

They sniffed the air. "It smells like they're this way!" said the thin mouse, starting to walk away from the castle and toward the trees where Delphie and Sugar were hiding.

"They're coming over here!" Delphie whispered in alarm.

Sugar looked dismayed. "I forgot that all of King Rat's mice love sugarplums! I'd better magic us away!"

But Delphie had noticed something. With the mice walking away from the castle, the door was unguarded. An idea popped into her mind. If they could just get the mice into the trees and away from the door for a few minutes . . .

"Wait!" she hissed as Sugar lifted her wand. "This could be our chance to get into the castle! Can you get me some more sugarplums—and fast?"

"It's too dangerous!" said Sugar as the mice approached the trees.

"Please!" Delphie begged.

Sugar hesitated and then pointed her wand at the ground. With a faint tinkle, a pile of sugarplums appeared.

Delphie picked up as many as she could. "Quick! Let's make a trail leading away from the castle!"

Sugar grabbed the remaining plums and they hurried through the trees. They placed one of the plums near the entrance to the woods, and then another and then another, all leading down the hill away from the castle. Delphie glanced around. Already she could hear the mice crashing through the woods! Sugar put the last plum where the woods ended in a steep bank that led into a shallow but fast-flowing stream.

Delphie suddenly had an idea of how to get the mice really out of the way. "If only we had some string."

"How about some ballet ribbon!" Sugar waved her wand and a big roll of pink ribbon appeared in her hand. "What do you want it for?"

"To hopefully get two mice very wet!" said Delphie, grinning.

She raced to the bank and tied one end of the ribbon around a tree on the left side and the other end around a tree on the right side. Then she smiled and grabbed Sugar's hand. "Come on! They mustn't see us."

She pulled Sugar back to the edge of the woods where there was a big bramble bush to hide behind just as the smaller mouse burst into sight.

"I found the sugarplum!" he exclaimed, snatching it up.

The tall one appeared just behind him. "There's another!" he cried, pouncing on the pale fruit. "And look! There are more of them!"

Peeping out from behind the bush,
Delphie and Sugar watched as the mice
began to run down the hill, scooping up the
sweet plums and squabbling over them.

"I saw that one first!"

"I want it!"

"No! I want it!"

The two mice were so busy jostling and
pushing each other that they didn't see the
ribbon stretched across the path until they
both tripped over it.

"Whoa!" shouted the mice, grabbing hold
of each other as they crashed to the ground.
Over and over they tumbled
down the bank until, with two
very loud splashes, they fell,
still shouting, into the stream.

Sugar gasped, looking half-shocked and half-delighted. "Oh, Delphie! You've made them so wet!"

Delphie grinned. "Maybe that'll teach them not to be so greedy in the future. Come on! Let's get inside the castle while they're busy drying off."

They raced toward the entrance. The wooden door had a huge metal handle in the shape of a rat's head. Delphie turned it and the door opened. On the other side there was an enormous empty hall with a stone fireplace. Above it there was a framed picture of a black rat with a crown on his head and a red cloak.

The Magic Ballet Shoes

On the far side of the room were two
towers of boxes, piled almost up to the
ceiling, with the word GLUE printed on
them.

"Look!" Sugar pointed to a table just in
front of the boxes. Standing on top of it was
a small painted wooden figure. He looked
like a soldier wearing a red
jacket with brass buttons, black
trousers and boots, and a sword
in his belt.

"It's the Nutcracker!" Delphie
said, running over and picking
the figure up.

But then she heard a noise. It sounded like
footsteps marching toward the door on the
left.

"Get back in the hall!" came a voice
outside the door. "You know King Rat said
the Nutcracker wasn't to be left on his own!
You call yourself a soldier! Coming to me
with ridiculous stories about smelling
sugarplums through the windows!"

"But I did, Sarge. I really did. I . . . "

"GET BACK IN THERE!"

"Quick!" Delphie gasped at Sugar. "There's
someone coming! We've got to hide!"

Dancing Magic

Delphie ran over and turned the handle of a door in the hallway. It opened into a small room that seemed to be used for keeping firewood. "In here!" She whispered.

Just as they were about to go in, Sugar waved her wand at the table. There was a tinkling sound as she magicked up another Nutcracker doll. "I'll put this on the table in front of the boxes so that they won't realize the real Nutcracker has gone."

Delphie and Sugar dived into the room and peeped back around the door just in time. Two mice hurried into the hall. One was dressed with boots and a sword like the mice outside had been. The other was wearing a vest with gold buttons. He looked very relieved when he saw the fake Nutcracker on the table in front of the boxes. "Lucky for you that the Nutcracker's still here. King Rat's been extremely pleased since he turned him into a toy.

"He was going to use the quick-drying glue in those boxes to stick all those horrible dancers to the ground, but he doesn't have to now. No one can dance while the Nutcracker's a prisoner here." He glowered at the other mouse. "So, stay where you are and don't let anyone past!"

The other mouse nodded and the sergeant strode out.

Sugar looked scared. "If that mouse stays outside the door, then we're trapped in here!"

"Maybe there's another way out." Delphie looked around. But there were no windows or other doors in the little room.

"If only we could bring the Nutcracker back to life, he would be able to help us fight our way out," Sugar said.

"Can't you use your magic to make him come alive again?" Delphie asked hopefully.

Sugar shook her head. "King Rat's powers

are too strong while we're inside the castle. Only really powerful magic will turn him back."

Suddenly Delphie heard Madame Za-Za's words from that afternoon echo in her head: *The real magic comes from telling a story and making the audience believe in that story. Never forget that—always believe in it.*

Delphie remembered how Madame Za-Za had looked straight at her while she had been speaking. It had been as if she had been talking directly to her. *Never forget that. . . .*

Maybe she'd been trying to tell her something. Delphie began to think hard. What happened in the story of *The Nutcracker* before the toy came to life?

Of course, she realized. *Clara dances with the*

toy Nutcracker. An idea grew in her head. Maybe if she danced with *this* Nutcracker he would come to life too!

Almost before the idea had formed in her mind, Delphie's feet began to tingle and in her head she heard the opening bars of the dance she had watched the girls doing that afternoon. Delphie moved forward into the opening pose. Holding her arms down low and with her left foot pointed forward in front of her, she looked down at the Nutcracker in her hands.

I'm Clara, she told herself. Then she began to do the dance she had been longing to do ever since the class that afternoon.

She skipped forward with tiny steps as if

she was floating across the floor. Stopping, she raised her hands, drew her right leg up against her left, and stretched it out behind her, staying perfectly balanced.

She gasped. The Nutcracker's arm had started to raise and his mouth to open. . . .

Sugar stared. "Your dance is bringing him to life! Dance some more, Delphie!"

Delphie didn't need any more urging. She moved into a pirouette, ran forward a few steps, then nimbly jumped into the air. She lifted the Nutcracker up high and spun around with him, her whole body glowing and tingling with the music as in her mind she became Clara dancing with her beloved doll.

There was a bright white flash. Delphie stopped with a gasp. The Nutcracker had come to life!

"Hello, Delphie," he said, smiling down at her.

Sugar threw her arms around him. "Oh, Nutcracker! Delphie's brought you back by dancing."

The Nutcracker nodded. "The strongest magic of all." He hugged her. "And now everyone in Enchantia will be able to dance again!" He looked at Delphie. "I can't thank you enough. You must have really believed in the dance to make the magic work." He took her hand. "Thank you," he said softly.

e grinned in delight.

Sug ran to the door. "We need to get out of here. Then I can use my magic to take us back to the village."

"Follow me!" The Nutcracker pulled out his sword and opened the door.

Escape!

The mouse who was standing guard by the table squeaked in surprise. "It's you!" He swung around and looked at the fake Nutcracker doll. "But . . . but . . . how can it be?"

The Nutcracker smiled. "Ballet magic," he said. "Let us past!"

"Oh no you don't," said the mouse, running

to stand between him and the front door. "You aren't getting away that easily!"

With one swift movement the Nutcracker danced forward and used his own weapon to flip the sword out of the mouse's grip. It flew into the air and landed with a clatter on the floor. With nothing to protect him, the mouse ran hastily backward. "Help! Help!" he shouted. "The Nutcracker's escaping!"

There was the sound of running footsteps. Then suddenly a door slammed open and a very loud voice boomed into the room.

"What is the meaning of this?"

The mice cringed and Delphie stared as a haughty black rat with red eyes walked into the room, flanked by four guards.

He was wearing a
purple cloak
trimmed with
white fur, and
he had a
golden crown
on his head.
He saw the
Nutcracker
and stopped.
"You!" he
exclaimed. "I
turned you into
a toy!"

"But now I have turned back!" cried the
Nutcracker. "And all of Enchantia will
dance again!"

"Not if I have anything to do with it!" King
Rat leaped forward, swiping his sword
viciously at the Nutcracker. His guards
closed in as well. Bravely, the Nutcracker
fought them off with strong, sweeping
strokes. But he was being beaten back.

"There are too many of them for the
Nutcracker to fight!" Sugar exclaimed as the
king and the guards advanced with their
swords. They began to back the brave
Nutcracker into the corner where the piles
of boxes marked GLUE were stacked. The
Nutcracker knocked against them and they
wobbled precariously.

Suddenly Delphie had an idea. She pulled
off one of her ballet shoes. "Stop it, King
Rat!" she shouted.

King Rat swung around. "Who are you?"

"Delphie!" She lifted the shoe up and hurled it at him.

King Rat ducked. "That's the oldest trick in the book!" he said as the shoe hit the boxes behind him. "Missed!"

"Oh no I didn't!" exclaimed Delphie as the pile of boxes began to sway.

The Nutcracker leaped nimbly out of the way, grabbing Delphie's ballet shoe from the floor as he did so, but King Rat was too busy laughing at Delphie to notice the boxes. "You missed! You did! You . . . "

His voice was drowned out as the boxes toppled over. They crashed down, jars of glue raining on his head. "Ow! Ooh! Ow!" he yelled.

The guards cried and shouted too. The jars smashed into each other as they fell, cracking open and covering King Rat and his soldiers in quick-drying glue.

King Rat pointed at Delphie, glue dripping down over his face and off his ears and whiskers. "Why, you . . . you . . . !"

But though he tried to run toward her, his feet were stuck!

"Come on," gasped Delphie, turning to Sugar and the Nutcracker. "Let's get out of here!"

And quickly they raced out of the castle and back to the woods.

"That was amazing, Delphie!" exclaimed Sugar.

"Fantastic!" said the Nutcracker, giving her her shoe back.

"We're free—that's the main thing." Delphie grinned as she put her shoe back on.

"And Enchantia should be returned to normal," said Sugar. "Come on, let's use my magic to get away from here and see what's happening!"

She waved her wand. Delphie found herself spinning around three times. When they landed she saw that they were in the village that she had seen painted on the scenery in the theater. The streets were full of characters from the ballet—toys, enormous sweets, dancers dressed up

as bright flowers, two Spanish dancers, and
a beautiful fairy in a rose-pink dress
dancing on her pointes.

Music was flooding magically through the
air. Sugar grabbed Delphie's hands. "Let's
dance!"

Holding lightly on to the Sugar Plum
Fairy's hands, Delphie felt herself being
swept up in the music—she didn't have to
stop to think what steps she was going to
do. As Sugar rose on to her pointes, Delphie
let the music guide her—she skimmed
across the ground with tiny steps and
jumped into the air, her arms outstretched,
her toes pointed. She landed softly and then,
with perfect balance, stretched one leg out
behind her. Delphie couldn't believe how

graceful she felt! It seemed like the music was flowing through her as she and Sugar ran forward together and pirouetted. The Nutcracker leaped in front of them, turning into a handsome prince as he landed. His glittering costume perfectly matched Sugar's. Delphie gasped as he swept the Sugar Plum Fairy up in his arms and lifted her high into the air. He turned and placed her down lightly. Holding on to his hand, she spun around on the tip of her toe. All around them the other characters danced too—the flowers waltzed, the snowflakes twirled, the Spanish dancers swung their tiered red skirts, and the Russian dancers linked arms. There was color and movement everywhere. The Nutcracker and Sugar came to a stop, their cheeks flushed, their eyes shining.

"It is almost time for you to go home, Delphie," the Nutcracker Prince said. "We can't thank you enough."

A thought struck Delphie. "I hope Mom and Dad don't wonder where I've gone!"

"Do not worry; time is different in our world and yours," said the Nutcracker Prince. "When you get back you will find that it is as if no time has passed at all."

Delphie felt relieved but also sad as she looked around at the enchanted world. "I don't want to leave here."

Sugar smiled at her. "You'll come back. You have the magic ballet shoes. Whenever we need you they will sparkle. If you put them on, they will bring you to Enchantia again." She danced over and kissed Delphie on both cheeks, then took out her wand. "This is to take home to remind you of us," she said, waving sparkles in the air.

Delphie gasped as a beautiful white tutu appeared in her hand. "Good-bye—and thank you," Sugar said. "Send my regards to Madame Za-Za." And with that she waved her wand over Delphie's head.

"Good-bye!" Delphie cried as the air around her swirled with color and she began to pirouette around and around . . . until suddenly she landed with a bump. . . .

Home Again

She was back in her bedroom sitting on her bed with a beautiful white tutu lying next to her.

Could my mom have put it there?

"Perhaps it was real after all," she whispered, her head spinning as she thought about everything that had just happened. She looked down at the ballet shoes on her feet and remembered Madame Za-Za's words: *They are very special shoes, Delphie. I hope one day you find out just how special they are. . . .*

Delphie could hardly believe it. As she began to unlace the ribbons, she thought about her ballet lessons. After her adventures in Enchantia, she was even more determined to practice really hard and get as good at ballet as she could. *After all, the better I am, the more I should be able to help in Enchantia,* she realized.

Delphie stood up and put the tutu and the shoes carefully on her bedside table. When would she next go to Enchantia and what would she have to do? She remembered what the Sugar Plum Fairy had said: *You have the magic ballet shoes. Whenever we need you they will sparkle. If you put them on, they will bring you to Enchantia again.*

Delphie hugged her arms around herself. She might not know when it was going to happen or for what she might be needed, but if the shoes glowed again, she would be there to help in whatever way she could!

Tiptoe over the page to learn
a special dance step. . . .

Darcey's Magical Master Class

Ballet Positions

Now it's your turn. Have fun!

Prepare
Put your heels together
with toes pointing outward.
Make an oval shape with
your arms.

First position
Now move your arms upward so
that your hands are in line with
your belly button.

Second Position
Move your feet to
hips-width apart
and open your arms.

Third position
Move your right foot
so that the heel touches the
middle of your left foot; sweep
your left arm in front of you.

Fourth position
Slide your right foot forward
and lift your left arm so it is
almost over your head.

Fifth position
Now bring both your
arms over your head.

Magic Ballerina
The Magic Spell

King Rat is up to his old tricks and has

cast a spell over all of Enchantia; can

Delphie help her friends before it's too late?

**Read on for a sneak preview
of book two. . . .**

Delphie landed with a bump to find herself in the same darkened theater, only this time the air was very cold. She jumped up eagerly and then caught her breath. It was all so different. The first time she had been here, there had been light and color. The scenery had shown mountains, fields, and a village as well as King Rat's castle, and there had been lots of characters on the stage, even though they had all been asleep.

But now the background scenery was just painted white and the stage was empty. The floor was covered in a thick blanket of snow. There were bare trees on the stage, their branches covered in icicles.

Delphie walked hesitantly toward the stage. "Sugar?" Her voice echoed through the empty theater. She didn't like this. There was a feeling in the air as if something was horribly wrong.

"Sugar!" she called uneasily. "Where are you? . . . "